THE DAY THE HICCUPS TOOK OVER

Jo Simmons

Illustrated by
Lee Cosgrove

For Jane, a champion knitter, with love

First published in 2023 in Great Britain by
Barrington Stoke Ltd
18 Walker Street, Edinburgh, EH3 7LP

www.barringtonstoke.co.uk

Text © 2023 Jo Simmons
Illustrations © 2023 Lee Cosgrove

A CIP catalogue record for this book is available
from the British Library upon request

ISBN: 978-1-80090-217-6

Printed in Great Britain by Charlesworth Press

CONTENTS

CHAPTER 1

It Started With a Hic!

It was Saturday morning, about eight o'clock. Frank was lying in bed. There was no need to rush. Frank had time before his trumpet exam, time before his swimming lesson. Time to relax and read his favourite magazine, *Knitting World*.

Frank turned the pages, admiring the amazing designs. There were knitted trousers, tiny hats for cats, even woolly cases for mobile phones.

Knitting was Frank's secret passion, his hidden talent. The scarf that he always wore he had knitted himself, but he'd told everyone he'd found it in the park. Frank had knitted mittens and socks and pencil cases, woolly ear warmers and cosy tea cosies. Knitting was his happy place.

On the cover of *Knitting World* was a photo of Eliot Abdi, the famous knitter from Kenya. No one knitted better than Eliot, or faster. He could knit a tank top in six minutes. A bobble hat in five, and the bobble itself took a fast forty seconds. Eliot was a knitting giant.

Frank turned the page to the interview. A quote from Eliot stood out:

"I have always been proud and open about my love of knitting, and I want to share my passion with the world."

That was all right for Eliot to say, Frank thought, but he had to keep his knitting quiet.

Everyone at school would laugh at Frank if they found out. Even his best friend Callum.

Since they had started Year Six, all Callum cared about was looking cool. Frank didn't dare tell him about his knitting hobby. Callum would laugh his socks off. All Frank wanted to do was knit, but he kept it a secret.

Frank read to the bottom of the page: "Eliot Abdi will be at the World Knitting Games at the Multiview Arena on the 15th of May."

That was today – and Frank had a ticket! He had saved up his pocket money, washed cars and walked his neighbour's dog Sponge every Saturday for six weeks to get it. Later that afternoon, he would be at the arena, seeing Eliot Abdi and all the other superstar knitters he admired so much in real life.

Frank closed his eyes and pictured it. The hall would be silent, as knitting events were always dead quiet. The audience would be transfixed by Eliot's flashing, dancing needles. No one would speak or even breathe as they watched Eliot work. Then – *TA DA!* – Eliot would hold up his latest knitted creation, and the crowd would go wild.

The thought made Frank grin, but his smile disappeared when something suddenly shoved him, hard.

Frank jolted forwards. He looked around, unsure about what had happened. He listened.

He waited. Nothing. He began to relax. Frank picked up his magazine again and …

There! Another jolt! And a loud HIC! This hic made his body bounce.

Frank leaped out of bed. The magazine fell to the floor. He suddenly understood. The jolts weren't coming from outside – they were coming from inside. They were hiccups.

"OK, no need to panic," Frank muttered. He'd had hiccups before. They normally went away after a few minutes. Most horrible things passed after a while, Frank told himself, like cramp or a Maths test or a bad haircut. But then …

HIC!

Frank laid his hands across his belly.

HIC! HIC! HIC!

The hiccups were speeding up. They were powerful too. Oddly powerful. It was like Frank was being punched from inside. Or as if a flea the size of a cocktail sausage was hopping around in his chest.

Frank had never experienced hiccups like this before. Some went HIC but others went HIC-ULCH. The ULCHes were the worst. They *hurt*!

HIC.

Frank decided to get dressed.

HIC.

The buttons on his shirt exploded out of his fingers with each hiccup. He put on a T-shirt instead.

Frank went downstairs for breakfast and poured milk over his cornflakes.

HIC.

The milk sploshed across the table.

He took a big gulp of juice.

HIC.

It spurted out of his mouth and sprayed the wall.

Frank swallowed a spoonful of cereal.

HIC.

The cereal leaped back into his mouth.

"Oh yuck," Frank said. He swallowed the mush again with a grimace.

And that's when Frank realised. That's when it hit him. These were not just any hiccups – these were *super-charged* hiccups!

"Morning, Frank," said his mum, dashing into the kitchen. She was wearing her headphones, music blasting out of them, and talking extra loud as a result. "I'm super busy today," she shouted. "I have got to get this jingle for Power Blast Toilet Cleaner finished. It's going to be very dramatic. Lots of cellos!"

Frank's mum wrote music for adverts and was always playing or composing. His dad was a fitness instructor and always outdoors.

HIC.

"What was that?" Frank's mum asked, but she didn't wait for a reply. "You have your trumpet exam at midday and then swimming, but first the dentist."

"The dentist? I didn't know anything about the dentist," Frank said.

"It's at eleven," Mum replied. "They're all nearby, so you'll be fine to go on your own, won't you? You're almost twelve after all."

Frank had no time to answer. His mum raced out to her recording studio in the garden.

Frank glanced at the clock.

HIC.

Frank's shoulders leaped up towards his ears.

Two hours until his dentist's appointment.

HIC.

His hiccups would be gone by then, wouldn't they?

CHAPTER 2

Hiccup Horrors

Back upstairs, Frank picked up his trumpet.
He tried to practise one of his exam pieces, but
the hiccups interrupted his breath. Instead
of smooth notes, Frank could only blast out
squeaks and parmps.

He made a face and put the trumpet down.
Two massive hiccups jolted inside him like a
double electric shock.

They'll go, Frank told himself. *They're only hiccups. Silly hiccups. Hang on, what even are hiccups?*

He picked up a book about the human body that his dad had given him. Dad was always swimming up waterfalls and running up mountains. He was big on health and fitness and, well, just big. Dad was like a door – a massive door with muscles.

Frank found the page on hiccups.

"The hiccup is actually a 'myoclonic jerk'," he read out loud.

"I'll feel like a myoclonic jerk if they don't stop soon," Frank muttered.

"They may sound like a chirp, squeak or 'hupp' and are a short but distracting interruption to breathing."

Frank hiccupped again. The book leaped in his hands.

"Distracting interruption?" Frank said. "More like being thumped on the inside by an angry toddler."

He read some more.

"If the hiccups don't pass in two hours, they may be classed as chronic and can become difficult to stop."

Frank frowned, puzzling over the meaning of the sentence. He gradually started to understand.

"I need to get rid of these hiccups soon, otherwise I'll be stuck with them for ever," Frank gasped. "Is that what this means? It is, isn't it?"

How long had he been hiccupping for already? An hour, maybe longer? Then Frank thought about the day ahead – dentist, trumpet exam, swimming, but, most serious of all, the World Knitting Games. Could Frank sit in the audience if he was hiccupping loudly? Would it put off Eliot Abdi? Would it ruin the show?

"I have to do something!" Frank said, jumping up with a wild look in his eyes. "Now! This minute! How do you stop hiccups? I know, hold your breath."

He pulled in a huge gulp of air and clamped his mouth shut. His lips were pressed tightly together. Frank didn't move. Slowly his face changed colour, from ham to baked bean to tomato. Still he held on, his eyes watering, his fists clenched, until he suddenly let the air out in a rush. He gasped in another full breath.

HIC.

A huge hiccup exploded from deep inside. Frank swayed. His eyes watered. He wiped his mouth nervously on his arm. He began jumping up and down but wasn't sure why.

Frank was tense. He was anxious. Perhaps bouncing like this would help.

Then he found himself running for the front door. He needed to move, race around, get out of breath, defeat his hiccups that way. Frank pulled on his trainers and yanked the front door open, hiccupping on the step. He dashed outside – straight into someone.

"Sorry, sorry," Frank said. He picked himself up and brushed his floppy hair out of his eyes. Now he could see who he had collided with. "Oh, it's you."

"Yes, it's me. The new girl from down the road."

She stood up and squinted at Frank.

"I'm in your class," the girl said. "You hang out with cool Callum, don't you? That's probably why you haven't spoken to me. I'm not cool enough. Anyway, I'm Daisy."

She thrust out her hand. Frank shook it. Daisy laughed.

"I didn't want a handshake, just for you to pass me my glasses," Daisy said. "They flew off when you hit me. Can you see them?"

"Oh yes, sorry," said Frank. He picked them up from the pavement and handed them to

Daisy. Then he hiccupped so hard he lurched to one side like he had been poked with a large, invisible stick.

"Ooh, nasty," Daisy said.

Frank nodded. "I've never had hiccups like this before. They are evil! I've got to get rid of them soon, or they might stay for ever. I read it in a book."

The words tumbled out of Frank's mouth, followed by a loud HIC.

"It's a disaster, and today of all days," he continued. "I've got a trumpet exam and a swimming trial and the dentist. But worse, much worse than all of that, I have to be somewhere later this afternoon. Somewhere really important, but it's quiet."

"The library?" Daisy said.

"No, an event. A special event, but not something you can go to if you're hiccupping like a drunk llama every thirty seconds!"

"What event?" Daisy asked.

"I can't tell you," said Frank. He was sure that Daisy would laugh if she knew it was the World Knitting Games.

"So what are you going to do?" she asked.

"Run," said Frank.

Daisy raised her eyebrows. "I'm not sure that will work. Why don't you come to my house, and we can look up hiccup cures on my brother's computer?"

"I haven't got time," said Frank, bouncing on the spot.

"But you *have* got time to run around the streets hiccupping like an *exploding* firecracker?" Daisy asked.

"Yes, no, sorry," said Frank, and then he was off, sprinting down the street.

Daisy watched him go. Frank ran fast, but every so often a hiccup made him ping up into

the air. Then he turned and ran back to her, jerking upwards with each new HIC.

"Changed your mind?" Daisy asked, smiling at him. "Want some help?"

Frank was about to say yes please, but he just said "HIC!" instead.

CHAPTER 3

Make Them Stop

"Look at this, Frank. It's going to be OK," Daisy said. She pointed at the laptop open on her kitchen table. "There are loads of cures for hiccups. A lot of them involve water. First, drink some ice water."

Daisy tumbled ice cubes into a glass. They cracked as the water from the tap trickled over them, then she passed the glass to Frank.

"Down in one," Daisy said.

He gulped it back and then stood still.

Nothing, nothing, nothing, then ...

HIC.

"OK," Daisy said. "It also says drink warm water."

She ran the hot tap and refilled Frank's glass.

He drank it. And then hiccupped.

"Don't panic," said Daisy. "Let's try the next thing on the list. Suck an ice cube." She went over to the freezer. "Oh, we've run out. I used the last ones in your water. But I've got some frozen peas. Open wide."

Frank opened his mouth and Daisy climbed onto a chair. (Frank was pretty tall and Daisy was pretty small.) She poured some frozen peas into Frank's mouth.

Frank sucked them for a while, his cheeks puffing out like a hamster eating sweetcorn. But then ... HIC.

A gigantic hiccup bounced out of him, forcing his mouth open and sending peas flying out. They skidded across the floor.

"Sorry," said Frank. They chased after the peas and picked them up. Then they tried the next cure on the list – drinking from the opposite side of the glass, upside down.

This just spilled the water all over Frank's face and hair, and made him splutter and cough.

"It also says try drinking water through a tea towel," said Daisy, draping one over the glass.

Frank took a couple of swigs. "It tastes fishy and horrible," he complained.

Daisy held up the tea towel and examined it.

"Oh, actually, that might be the one we use to wipe out the cat's bowl."

Frank slumped to the floor, his back against the fridge, his head in his hands.

"Don't give up, Frank," Daisy said. "We can try something else. Quickly, lie on your back."

"What are you going to do, sit on me?" Frank mumbled. Then he hiccupped for the gazillionth time that morning.

"That's exactly what I'm going to do, to compress your chest," Daisy said.

Frank lay flat and Daisy sat on him, but within seconds he was hiccupping again. Each time he hiccupped, Daisy pinged up, like she was riding a trotting pony.

"Give me your hand," she said.

"I don't want to hold hands," Frank moaned, beginning to feel hopeless.

Daisy grabbed his hand anyway and began pressing down on Frank's palm.

"Ouch," he protested. "First you sit on me, now you're trying to break my thumb."

"It's a pressure point," Daisy said. Her black eyebrows sank beneath her glasses as she pushed harder and harder. "It's supposed to help."

"Hurt more like," Frank grumbled, and then HIC!

Daisy dropped his hand, but she wasn't done yet.

"Stick your tongue out," she said, sounding very bossy now. "Frank, I'm trying to help. Do it!"

Frank poked his tongue out a little, and Daisy grabbed it and pulled.

"Ow! What are you doing?" Frank yelled, but it came out more like "Wam wam woo wooming?"

"It's another possible cure," Daisy said. But then she pulled a face and let Frank's tongue go,

realising what she was doing. She wiped her
hand on his top.

Frank hiccupped and then moaned, "None of
this is helping, and I'm running out of time. And
you're heavy. How can someone so small be so
solid? Can you get off, please? I've drunk loads

of water in the last twenty minutes. If I hiccup again, I will definitely pee myself."

Daisy jumped up, and Frank ran to the loo. When he got back to the kitchen, she was at the computer again, studying another website.

"What took you so long?" Daisy asked.

"There was a lot," Frank said. "I had to be careful too. It's not easy to pee while you're hiccupping."

Daisy held up her hand in a stop sign.

"Too much information," she said. "Now look, here are some other ideas. Suck a lemon. I don't have any lemons, but I've got this."

She passed Frank a potato. He took a tiny bite and then gave it a tentative suck. Then Frank hiccupped.

"Maybe it needs to be a sharp flavour," Daisy said. "I know – an onion."

She found one and peeled off its brown papery skin.

"If I lick it, promise me you won't grab my tongue again," Frank said.

"I promise I will never grab *anyone's* tongue again," Daisy replied. "It was gross."

Frank licked the onion, made a face and hiccupped.

"Gah!" he shouted, and threw the onion in the bin.

"OK, look, it's all right," said Daisy. "There is one more cure to try."

"Do I have to gargle with cooking oil or lick a fish finger or something?" Frank asked.

"No, it's a good one. Trust me," Daisy said. She rummaged in a cupboard and pulled out a bag. "This is granulated sugar. You have to swallow some."

29

She passed Frank a spoon. He dug it into the bright white granules, then popped it into his mouth. The sugar crunched under his teeth and grew soggy on his tongue. Sweetness filled his mouth, and for the first time that day Frank began to relax.

"I might have some of that too," Daisy said, dipping her own spoon in. They sat at the kitchen table, eating sugar, not speaking, enjoying the quiet and the sweet, syrupy flavour. Frank finally felt calm.

"That's a nice scarf," Daisy said. She picked up the scarf Frank was wearing, which had stripes in deep red and pink.

"I made it myself," Frank said, without thinking. He was so relaxed, he forgot to keep his knitting a secret.

"Great," said Daisy.

"Really?" said Frank. "You don't think it's funny or weird that I knit?"

"Why would I? This scarf is so beautiful," Daisy said. "You're talented."

"When I knit, it's like there's this calm that comes over me," Frank said, leaning forwards. "I'm in the zone, and my hands seem to be

working without me having to tell them what to do. You know?"

Daisy nodded.

"I get that when I eat crisps," she said. Daisy pretended she was dipping her hand into a crisp packet over and over again. "I'm joking. I think knitting sounds cool. It's your passion."

"You're the first person I've told," Frank said, smiling shyly.

"Your parents don't know that you knit? You should tell them. What about Callum?"

Frank shook his head.

"He'd just laugh at me," he said.

Frank dipped his spoon into the sugar again and then paused, realising something. He tapped Daisy on the knee. He pointed at his chest. Daisy watched him for a while and then her eyes grew as huge as dinner plates.

"Oh wow," she whispered. "You haven't hiccupped. It's working."

Frank held one finger up, listening. He didn't dare believe it.

The seconds ticked past with nothing – no jolt, no hic, no lurch. Frank began to smile. His eyes sparkled. He leaped up and hugged Daisy hard.

"Daisy, you're a genius!" he said. "Thank you, thank you, thank you."

"You're cured, Frank!" Daisy shouted.

Frank punched the air, then he noticed the clock.

"And I'm also late for the dentist. Got to run. Thanks again!"

CHAPTER 4

Disaster at the Dentist's

Frank arrived in the waiting room just as Dr Dudley the dentist appeared. He greeted Frank cheerfully.

"Good to see you, young man. Come this way. Take a seat."

Frank followed Dr Dudley into his room and hopped into the dentist's chair.

"Any problems?" Dr Dudley asked.

"None at all," said Frank. "In fact, I just got rid of terrible hiccups."

"Ah, I meant problems with your teeth," said Dr Dudley. "But that's great too. Always good to be hiccup-free before a visit to the dentist. I wouldn't want to get nipped."

He chuckled and lowered the chair down.

Frank opened his mouth, thinking how friendly and nice Dr Dudley was. He always made coming to the dentist pleasant. But then ... a single, violent punch blasted out of Frank.

HIC!

The hiccups had suddenly returned!

Maybe it was because Frank was lying backwards. Maybe it was because his mouth was open. We may never know. But this hiccup was the biggest yet – a huge jolt that seemed to lift Frank's whole body off the chair. Dr Dudley pulled his hands clear just in time.

"They're back!" Frank wailed. "How can they be back?"

"Not to worry, Frank," Dr Dudley said. "Perhaps that was a one-off." He chuckled again. He laughed about everything, which was why Frank felt so bad when this happened ...

Dr Dudley leaned in again with his mirror and pointy metal toothpick. He reached towards the back of Frank's mouth, but then, with no warning, Frank's body rocked and his mouth slammed shut like a trapdoor. HIC-ULCH!

"Owwww!" wailed Dr Dudley. He pulled his hand out and waved one finger in the air. Frank noticed it looked red and had teeth marks in it.

"I'm sorry, I'm so sorry," Frank said. He leaped up, his cheeks bright red with embarrassment.

The nurse was examining Dr Dudley's finger now. Feeling upset and horrified, Frank did the only thing he could think to do. He bolted.

"Do you need to book another appointment?" the receptionist shouted as Frank raced past. All he wanted to do was get away – far away. Frank didn't stop until he had made it to the park, where he paused by the tennis courts and bent over, panting.

HIC.

Another big hiccup rocked him. It forced him upright, like a cork flying out of a bottle. Frank was so disappointed he started banging his chest with his fist, hopping about and muttering, "Go away, go away!"

"Hi, Frank," said a voice.

Frank stopped punching himself suddenly. It was his friend Callum – cool Callum to everyone else.

"I was watching you jumping about and talking to yourself," Callum said. "Pretty weird. What's wrong with you?"

"Hiccups," said Frank.

"How bad are they?" Callum asked.

"Bad," said Frank. *Just wait, you'll see*, he thought. Sure enough, another whopper burst up from the depths of Frank's body.

"Woah! Those are awesome," said Callum, grinning with delight. "Your whole body shook. Hey, why don't you go and hiccup in front of those kids over there? See what they do."

Callum pointed to some toddlers in the sandpit.

"I'm not sure ..." Frank said.

"Go on, it'll be hilarious," said Callum.

Frank slowly walked towards the children and stood near them. Soon, a noisy hiccup blew up – one of the HIC-ULCH ones. Two toddlers jumped with surprise. One of the toddlers stared up at Frank with a blank face and then burst into tears. Another threw sand at him and called him a "silly sausage".

Frank went back to Callum, who was laughing and slapping his thigh.

"Brilliant!" Callum said. "Let's see who else you can freak out with your massive weird hiccups. How about that old lady who's asleep on the bench?"

"I don't think that's a good idea," Frank said.

"No, it's not a good idea – it's a totally brilliant idea," Callum said. He gave Frank a shove.

Frank walked slowly forwards. Callum waved his hands for Frank to go nearer, watching eagerly. Frank stepped closer and then HIC!

The woman jolted awake. She put her hand over her chest, gasping for breath. She looked up at Frank.

"You could have given me a heart attack," she said. "What are you thinking, standing next to frail old ladies and jerking them awake with your horrible sounds?"

"It's hiccups," Frank said.

"It's *dangerous*," said the old lady. She picked up her walking stick and jabbed it at Frank.

He mumbled "Sorry" as he backed away. Then Frank went to find Callum, who was doubled over because he was laughing so much.

"Let's do that again," Callum said, wiping tears of glee from his eyes.

"I can't," Frank said, walking off. "I have to go to my trumpet exam."

Callum didn't take the hint. He followed Frank, shouting "Woah" and "Nice one" and "Massive" every time he hiccupped. Frank didn't appreciate Callum's commentary. Why was he finding this so amusing? Wasn't he supposed to be Frank's friend?

They walked past the Multiview Arena. Signs for the World Knitting Games were everywhere. Callum paused and grinned, pointing at them.

"That sounds like the worst thing ever, doesn't it?" Callum said. "Like, *so* boring."

"Yeah," said Frank. He tried to sneer along with Callum, while also trying not to cry. Frank so wanted to be there, to present his hard-earned ticket at the gate and take his seat for an amazing knitting display. But with hiccups like his? Noisy, ugly hiccups? Forget it.

"I really have to go now," said Frank.

"Fine, OK," Callum said. "Good luck with your trumpet exam. That'll be fun with hiccups like that." But Frank was already jogging away.

CHAPTER 5

Not Waving But Drowning

Back at his house, Frank picked up his trumpet and then grabbed some cotton wool from the bathroom. He caught sight of himself in the mirror. His shoulders hopped up with every hiccup, his floppy hair messy, his eyes a bit wild.

Frank touched his knitted scarf. It was the only thing that looked unchanged by these never-ending hiccups. Perhaps the scarf would bring him luck, or at least comfort. Then Frank ran to the church hall down the road where his trumpet exam was taking place.

THE DAY THE HICCUPS TOOK OVER

Jo Simmons

Illustrated by
Lee Cosgrove

Barrington Stoke